Party in Catland

Alice Goyder

CHATTO & WINDUS · LONDON

One day, after school, Tilly said to Minnie,
'Let's have a party!'
'If only we could,' said Minnie,
'I shall ask Mother,' said Tilly.

'If you are a good little kitten,' said Mother Grimalkin, 'and help me with my sewing, you and Minnie shall have a party!'

Tilly said she would write the invitations. But there were so many to do, her wrist quite ached and Mother Grimalkin had to help her.

Tilly and Minnie had to dust and sweep the house from top to bottom so that everything should be spick and span for the party.

Mother Grimalkin gave Tilly a blue silk sash to tie round her waist and a ribbon for her neck and a beautiful Chinese fan.

Little Kitty Catkin was the first guest
to arrive. She wore a brand new party shawl.

'What shall we play?' said Minnie when all the guests had arrived. 'I know,' cried Tilly. 'Let's play Hunt the Slipper!'

After Hunt the Slipper there was dancing.
They waltzed and whirled and jigged
and capered and then it was time for tea.

What a spread it was! Mother Grimalkin had baked a big fruit cake with thick, white icing and everybody laughed and ate and laughed and ate.

After tea, they had theatricals. Tilly played Little Red Riding Hood and Minnie played the Big Bad Wolf.

That night Tilly dreamed of play-acting and dancing and Hunt the Slipper and, as sometimes happens in dreams, the slipper turned into a mouse.

Published by
Chatto and Windus Ltd
40 William IV Street, London WC2N 4DF

*

Clarke, Irwin & Co Ltd, Toronto

Edited, designed and produced by
Culford Books
135 Culford Road, London N1

First published 1978

ISBN 0 7011 2349 4

Printed and bound by
Waterlow (Dunstable) Ltd, England